For Emily, Lucy, Olivia,
Daisy and Bethany ~ J C

For Nick, Edie and Lilie ~ K D

LITTLE TIGER PRESS LTD,
an imprint of the Little Tiger Group
1 Coda Studios, 189 Munster Road, London SW6 6AW
www.littletiger.co.uk

First published in Great Britain 2019
Text copyright © Josephine Collins 2019
Illustrations copyright © Kirsti Davidson 2019
Josephine Collins and Kirsti Davidson have asserted their rights to be identified as the
author and illustrator of this work under the Copyright, Designs and Patents Act, 1988
A CIP catalogue record for this book is available from the British Library

FAIRYTALE CLASSICS

Sleeping Beauty

Josephine
Collins

Kirsti
Davidson

LITTLE TIGER
LONDON

Once upon a time, there were a King and a Queen who had everything in the world, except for a child.

When, at last, Princess Aurora was born,
the King jumped for joy and announced:
"It's time to celebrate!"

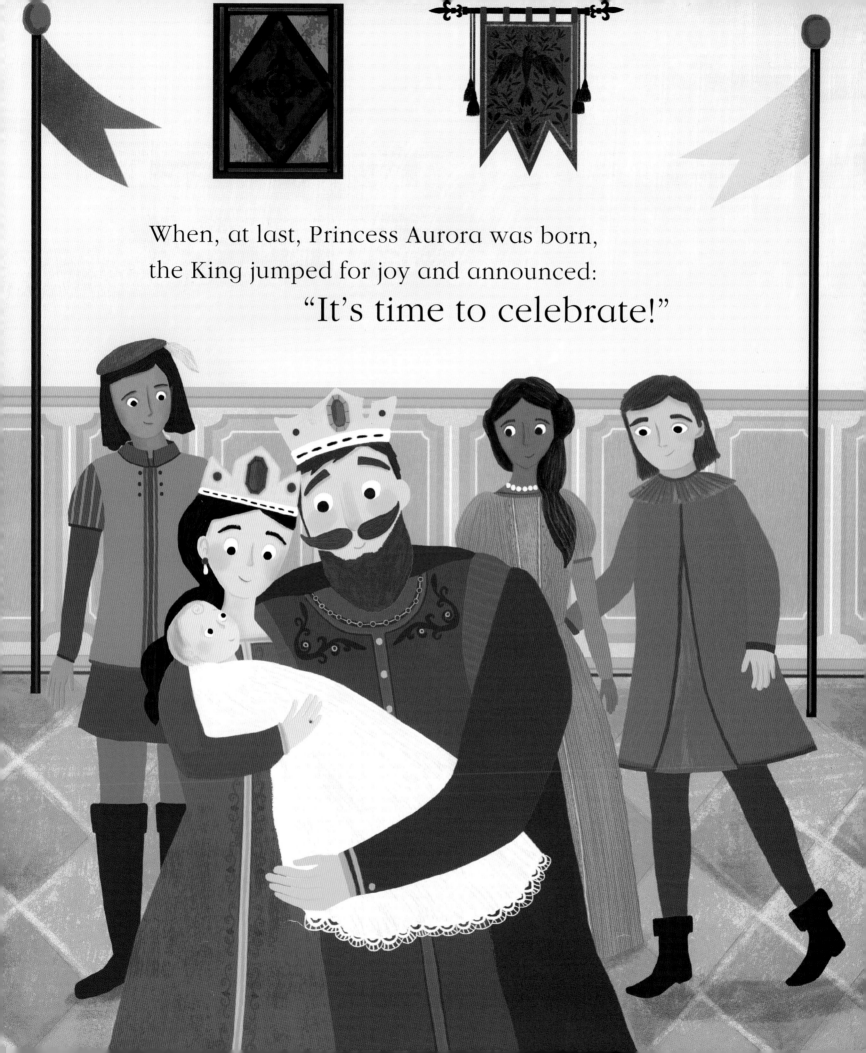

He organised a magnificent ball.
The fairies who lived in the
kingdom would be the star guests.
But in his excitement, the King
carelessly forgot to invite one of them.

When the fairies arrived at the glittering party, they gave baby Aurora their gifts of wisdom, beauty, courage and everything a Princess could wish for.

But **suddenly**, the forgotten fairy thundered in . . .

"How dare you forget me!" she screeched. "On her fifteenth birthday, the Princess shall prick her finger on a spindle and die!" And she stomped out.

Everyone looked in horror at the final fairy, who still had her gift to give, hoping she could help.

"I cannot remove this curse, but I can help the Princess," she said. "When she pricks her finger, she will not die. Instead she will fall asleep for **one hundred** years!"

After that, up and down the land,
the King ordered that spindles be destroyed.
Everyone obeyed.

The years passed, and Aurora grew up to be just as **clever,** **brave** and **beautiful** as the fairies had promised.

When the Princess turned fifteen, the palace celebrated with a party.

During a very long game of hide-and-seek, Aurora stumbled upon a door she had never seen before.

"How did I miss that?" she gasped, and pushed open the door to explore.

Down,

down,

down

twisted a shadowy winding staircase . . .

Whirr, whirr, whirr! came a strange sound from the room ahead.

Suddenly, there in front of her was an old woman, spinning.

"Excuse me, but what is that?" Aurora asked,
pointing at the spinning wheel.
   "Why don't you have a little try?" said the woman,
with a sly smile, for she was the forgotten fairy!

But no sooner had Aurora
touched the spindle,
than she pricked
her finger . . .

and fell down
into a
deep,
deep
sleep.

And the King and Queen
in their throne room . . .

the servants in the halls . . .

the horses in the stables,
the pigeons on the roof . . .

and even the dogs in the yard –
all fell fast asleep too.

Years passed, and a thick hedge of thorns grew in a tangle around the palace, hiding it from the world.

Brave Princes who had heard the tale of the sleeping Princess would try to find the palace . . .

but each one soon
gave up and ran
back home.

Then one day, exactly one hundred years
after the wicked spell had been cast,
a lucky Prince arrived in the Kingdom.

As he hacked at the sharp thorns,
they suddenly transformed into
beautiful flowers and let him pass.

"I can't understand what those other Princes were moaning about!" the Prince smiled, and trotted off to find the Princess.

Past the sleeping
pigeons, horses and
dogs he skipped . . .

past the sleeping servants and the
sleeping King and Queen he crept . . .

down,
down,
down
the winding stairs he went, until he came to the room where Princess Aurora lay asleep.

The Princess's beauty left the Prince
speechless. He instantly fell in love.

He couldn't resist taking her in
his arms and kissing her. And the
moment his lips touched hers . . .

the Princess woke up!
And so did everyone in the palace!

"At last!" Princess Aurora gasped.
"I was beginning to think no one was
ever going to rescue me! Right, I
think it's time to party!"

The King threw the biggest, glitziest party ever, and this time he was careful not to leave anyone out by accident. He did, however, leave one particular fairy off his invitation list on purpose! Princess Aurora and her Prince lived happily ever after, and luckily . . .

the forgotten fairy was
never seen again!